Erotic Fantasies Collection

Vol. 1

Erika Sanders

Erotic Fantasies Collection

Erika Sanders

Series

Erotic Fantasies Collection Vol. 1

This book consists of the following fantasies:

1 - Fantasy in the park

2 - Married and dissatisfied woman

3 – My boyfriend's father

4 – Fantasy with strangers

5 – Infidelity with mature

Erotica Fantasies Collection , a series of novels with high romantic and erotic taboo content.

(All characters are 18 years or older)

Index:

EROTIC FANTASIES COLLECTION
ERIKA SANDERS

FANTASY IN THE PARK

It was Saturday and usually there is no action in my Colonia, so I decided to go for a walk in the park in the neighboring Colonia, to see what fishing there was, since that park had a reputation that you can hook up very easily there.

I dressed very sexy and flirty and got ready to head towards the park, it was a bit far to walk so I requested an Uber.

The driver already knew me because I had previously requested services from him, so I confidently sat in the seat of the front passenger.

I asked him to take me to the park and we started talking. The truth is, I looked super sexy, almost irresistible he he , so the boy started talking in an off-color manner, there was a moment when he got excited and put his hand on my leg, as I was wearing a skirt, because my pantyhose could be seen. .

So we were talking, he already wanted to put his hand on me and to tease him I opened my legs a little, he started caressing my sex over my panties... But that's another story, it ends here because we had already arrived at the park so I got off, I was going to pay him, but he refused, he warned me that next time. If you want to know what happens next, don't miss this series of erotic fantasies.

I bought a delicious ice cream and proceeded to take a walk around the park to let myself be seen and see if I could get anything.

I walked like that for a while until a mature man approached me and started talking to me. You already know that my delirium is the mature ones, so I accepted willingly.

We were talking very fun, suddenly he asked me my age, and I told him I'm 19. I really look older, because I'm very developed, since I was 13 I've already awakened low passions, but I'll tell him about that later.

With a shy voice and flirtatious look I asked him, how many do you have? 23 responded.

I was surprised because his appearance clearly shows that he is an older man, at least 60, did I tell him how? You look a little older.

He smiling slyly told me 23 cm... he he ...

I turned all red, nervous and swallowing saliva as soon as I managed to say ah!

The funny guy kept provoking me and looking me directly in the eyes he shamelessly asked himself, how many of you do you like?

I turned red again and even more nervous, but I tried to hide it and told him, "Actually, I like older people," I said, a bit flirtatious.

He smiled amused and told me, what do you think if we go to the cinema, they are showing a very good movie, smiling maliciously, I readily accepted and we headed towards the cinema that was close by.

The cinema only shows porn movies, I already knew that because I once went on a getaway with some friends from Cole, but I'm going to tell you about that later, in another publication.

It is already known that in those cinemas the place is almost completely dark, you can barely notice the illuminated signs for the bathrooms, so it lends itself to all kinds of maneuvers if you are up for it.

And of course I was up for it.

It didn't take long for the man to put an arm behind me, I approached him and, delicately kissing my cheek, he began to caress my boobs. That made me very nervous, and I looked everywhere to check if no one was seeing us, in reality, no one could see us in that darkness, so I tried to relax and let myself do it.

The man managed to take my boobs out of my clothes and started sucking them. Immediately my nipples stood up and became super hard, which he immediately noticed and he groped me more and more and sucked me in such a way that I was already super excited.

Suddenly he put his hand on my leg and as I already told you, because of the little skirt I was wearing, my legs and panties could be seen. Immediately and automatically, I spread my legs and adjusted myself so that he could enjoy himself.

He started to grope me, and as soon as I felt his fingers rubbing my sex, I couldn't resist, I spread my legs further and grabbed his cock over his pants and started stroking it very well.

He put his hand in my sex and noticed how I was already all wet, he got excited and put his fingers in me as much as he could, I had to stand on my legs to facilitate his maneuver, when I felt him touch my clitoris, it became hard and well standing waiting to receive more, I was super excited, I bent down towards him and started sucking his cock, he was also already very excited, I felt how it was growing with each suck of mine, I realized that the 23 cm that He had told me they weren't lies.

Things were already getting worse, when suddenly she took my hand and took it off of her cock, she took her hand out of my sex and in a soft voice, but she seemed super excited, let's go she told me.

I immediately knew what was going to happen and without waiting for him to repeat it to me, I didn't bother and got up and we left there.

We crossed the street and immediately went to a little motel that was near the cinema.

Without saying a word we undressed and without wasting time I pounced on him and prepared to continue with the cock sucking that I was giving him in the cinema, he thanked me by spreading my legs and putting his face between my sex, which by then I was super wet, my clitoris was wet and stood up longing to be tasted by a tongue.

We did 69 for several minutes until my whore, I got on top of his cock and with one pull I put in the 23 cm of cock that he had promised me, I almost came from the excitement and lust that filled me.

So we spent a good while fucking in various positions, when I realized that he was going to come, I immediately got on all fours with my back to him and like the true whore that I am, I shamelessly offered him my ass.

He didn't hesitate for a second, he filled me with saliva and just from feeling his enormous head enter me, I made a moan of pain, lust, excitement and I started to move like crazy, provoking him and begging for more cock.

He no longer had mercy on me and he stuck the rest of his cock that was left outside into my ass. It made me scream in pain, but instead of getting away, I squeezed my ass and began to move wildly. We stayed like that for a while until It made me come tremendously, when he realized that, he couldn't hold it any longer and came inside me filling me all with his boiling milk.

It was the first time I swallowed a 9 inch cock, and I promise you that wasn't the last time or the last big cock I fucked.

MARRIED AND DISSATISFIED WOMAN

I am a model housewife, young, beautiful, sexy, with a good body, married and unfaithful, that kind of girl that all married people dream of.

But it turns out that my husband is also very young, but he is, without any experience. And I'm not interested in teaching him anything. So we are married, but nothing about sex and the truth is, thanks to my dad, I am completely sure that I was born for that, to have sex, to fuck like crazy, and the truth is that I really don't care who, The point is to fuck and give pleasure to the body, ufff.

The time came when my friends at school started calling me Random Girl because of the amount of things that had happened to me, most of them about sex.

Once I went to the movie theater with my husband, it was half full and a little dark, so we couldn't see well if there were places for us, so we stayed leaning on the little bar that faces the aisle to the back of the seats.

That's how we were, when suddenly, a guy started rubbing me from behind, with some dissimulation, so that my husband wouldn't notice. I didn't want to say anything either so he wouldn't find out.

So for a long time after he was rubbing his cock between my legs, as I didn't say anything, he got excited and started caressing my buttocks surreptitiously, over my dress.

Those who have followed me for a long time know that I always go out dressed super sexy, for whatever might be offered, of course. Either with a short skirt and a blouse with a neckline. Or like this time, a short tight dress with a neckline. The fabric of my dress allows me to touch you and feel like you are almost touching my body, that fabric is that rich, that's why I love wearing dresses like that.

Well, imagine what the boy felt when he was groping me, he could almost feel my body in all its splendor.

At that moment my husband told me that there was an unoccupied place, that I should go sit down, I told him, don't worry, I'm fine here, you better go over there, and so he did.

The boy understood that I was going to let him continue touching me and his caresses began to become more and more daring, and like the good whore that I am, he let me.

I lifted my dress until my bare buttocks and panties were visible. He began to caress them, very horny. When he got too horny, he took out his cock and, naked, leaned against me, taking me by the waist and started rubbing it in the middle of my buttocks.

How delicious that hot and throbbing cock felt between my buttocks, and he also leaned against me and rubbed me very well. Shortly after, he separated my panties and began to rub his cock directly on my sex, by which time I was already super wet.

I turned around towards him and leaned with my back to the bardita, I put my panties aside, I took his cock and I myself began to rub my sex with his cock.

It didn't take long, when the boy took my boobies out of my dress and started sucking them, my nipples became super hard and well positioned, that's a sign that I'm already very horny, at that point everything, absolutely everything It's been worth it to me, mother.

I took his cock and placed it in my sex, I grabbed his waist and pulled him towards me, in a clear sign that he should put it in me. He didn't wait long, pulling me by the waist and bending down a little, he put his entire cock into my sex, which was already completely wet, so it wasn't difficult for him to put it in.

That was delicious, forbidden sex is the best and cannot be compared to anything, imagine, fucking in the cinema, full of people, with my husband nearby, and the boy with a hot, huge, thick and big-headed cock, just the way I like them, just the way my dad gets used to them.

We were only like this for a few minutes, the boy made me finish with squirts, I made a tremendous effort not to scream, although some moans of pleasure, of lust, of fever came out, I clung to the boy, pressing myself hard against his cock and that was enough. so that it released tremendous jets of milk. I couldn't stand standing any longer, my legs buckled and I knelt in front of him, I took advantage of that moment to suck him really good and clean him properly, as it should be...

The moment the boy left, my husband returned because he was about to finish the movie and we hugged each other to take the bus to our house.

MY BOYFRIEND'S FATHER

That day I was feeling a little excited, which is very strange because I always have a lot of ha ha, so I decided to visit my boyfriend and give him a little surprise. To get home. I knocked and his dad opened it to me. Hello, love, he told me, come in, my son is not here, but he will be back soon. I passed with complete confidence because he already knew me since high school, apart from that I had a lot of trust in him and I knew that he appreciated me a lot.

I went to the living room and I was surprised to see that he was drinking with a friend of his, I don't know why I had assumed that he was alone. The fact is that I said hello and they sat me in the middle of the two, as always, my skirt went up and showed my beautiful thighs, and as always, I did nothing to lower my skirt, among other things, I love that men see me and if they are mature, then better. And at that moment I was sitting between two mature men with my skirt up to my thighs.

Apparently they didn't give any importance to that and told me that they were watching a porn movie, that if I wanted to see it or they would change it. That didn't really bother me so I told him it was fine, it's no problem for me.

They offered me a drink and I accepted, I felt that the drink they gave me was a bit strong, but at 18 I wasn't going to act stupid, so I didn't say anything and I drank it. The truth is, I don't drink much alcohol and that drink makes me dizzy almost immediately. The worst thing is that they offered me another one and again I accepted it and again I felt dizzy.

I didn't say anything, I stayed looking at the screen, the movie had already gotten very hot, there were two older men enjoying a young girl. At that moment it dawned on me, I was alone with two older men!!! and the drink, the truth is that I was already getting horny, I felt a little embarrassed to feel that way next to those men and one of them was my boyfriend's father. I felt a little nervous. I felt worse when my boyfriend's father put an arm behind my shoulders, came a little closer and told me that I had already become very beautiful. As embarrassed as I was by the alcohol and how horny I felt, I only managed to lean my head on the back of the sofa and looking into his eyes I said thank you. He took my face with one hand, I was super nervous, because apart from everything, that man had always seemed very attractive to me despite his age. The two men were probably around 60 years old if not older. I didn't know what to do and the only thing I could think of was to close my eyes as I felt his huge hand on my face, it felt warm, very delicious.

The man dared and planted a
tremendous kiss on my mouth, which
took me by surprise, I got super nervous,
I didn't know what to do, I was very
quiet when to my surprise, I opened my
mouth so he could kiss me at will. , and
not only that, but I gave him my tongue,
you know what that means, it means
that you are horny and that you give
yourself over to him for whatever he
wants.

Well, what he wanted was to reach
under my blouse and caress my breasts.
You already know how I get when
someone touches my tits. Immediately
my nipples stopped and became super
hard. He realized and knew that this was
the signal for the next step. The next
step was that he started sucking my
nipples. Instead of walking away from
there, seeing how dangerous this was
already getting and my boyfriend wasn't
coming, I only managed to separate my
legs and put a hand on his enormous

bulge that was already visible under his pants.

He accepted my delivery and began to put his hand between my legs, I only managed to separate them more. Seeing this, the friend perked up and started sucking my nipples too. That really turned me on, having two older men putting their hands on me and sucking my nipples, one on each side, it's not something to stay still, that especially drives me crazy. So, without thinking about it, I placed my other hand on the other man's penis and began to caress them both. They immediately dropped their pants and took out their cocks so I could caress them to my liking, which I did without any problem.

The bastards had enormous cocks, big, thick and big-headed, just the way I like them and I got ready to enjoy them, touching each of them with each hand, while they continued indulging themselves by sucking my nipples. If you can imagine that scene, you will understand that I was already more than horny. My boyfriend's dad sat on the arm of the couch and offered me his huge cock, which I immediately accepted without thinking, I got on all fours on the couch and leaned on that beautiful cock and started sucking it, off, It tasted delicious, huge, hot and it excited me how it throbbed inside my mouth. The other man took advantage and got under me, removed my panties and started licking my sex, which by then is already super wet. The man took pleasure in sucking my clit and drinking my juices. I was already more than prepared for what was coming.

They got up from the position they were in on the couch and my boyfriend's dad lay down on his back in a clear sign that I should mount him and so I did. I settled on his belly and, taking his cock, I placed it on my sex and in one go I put it up to my balls, I became frantic and started moving like crazy, how I loved that cock, it felt huge, hot, I It filled everything. The other man approached me from behind and lifting my buttocks, he filled me with saliva from behind and without saying water, he put his huge cock up my ass, I moaned in pain, he took it out a little, he adjusted it to me better and I started to move my ass, that was the signal for him to put it all in me from behind in one go. I moaned, sighed and moved like crazy. Can you imagine what it's like to be locked in front and behind by two beautiful cocks of two mature studs? That's a dream for any hot schoolgirl. And at that moment I was already making it happen. So you will understand all the lust that was present at that moment. I was unrestrained, moving like the true slut that I am, and I'm not ashamed to admit it. Of all the female friends at my school, I am the sluttiest and I love that. And everyone knows that.

There was a moment when the two men exchanged positions, and they slammed into me again, making me feel like the happiest woman in the world at that moment. Not only do you have to know how to be a whore and give yourself to anyone, it is also important to know how to enjoy a good fuck, and at that moment I was enjoying two excellent fucks at the same time.

I couldn't take it anymore and I came tremendously splashing everywhere. Seeing that, the two men attacked harder until they finished inside me, one from the front and the other from behind, filling me with boiling milk on both sides. Making your man come is a source of satisfaction for one, but making two men come inside you at the same time is priceless.

Well, my boyfriend never arrived and I was grateful for that, I would have hated if they had interrupted us in that tremendous double fuck.

Of course, those visits to my boyfriend's house when he was away were repeated many times.

FANTASY WITH STRANGERS

On one occasion, my boyfriend invited
me to his house for a meeting with
friends, something that was very
common and that we did regularly, to
which I readily accepted.

Usually at those meetings, at one point,
my boyfriend and I sneak off to have a
quick fuck and then return to the
meeting. Everyone knew that and almost
everyone did the same.

On that occasion, what surprised me was
that there were only boys, no women
and all of them were complete strangers
to me. Even so, I didn't say anything, and
we started drinking and talking
pleasantly.

At one point, they played soft music, very pretty, kind of horny, like what you listen to when you start to fuck.

The fact is that no one danced because they were pure men. Suddenly, my boyfriend asked me to dance a little for them, to liven up the meeting, for which everyone applauded, celebrating the idea, and I just got ready to give them a show.

She was wearing a short, tight dress, one of those that I love, and that one in particular made me look super sexy, super beautiful, super horny and super slut. That's the idea of wearing one of those dresses to meetings.

They dimmed the lights a little and I started to move really sensually, since I was a girl I had developed very well, but now, at 18, I had a spectacular body, and an angelic and innocent face, with a smile and a look that melted everyone. any.

So I was moving alone for a bit, suddenly a boy came up and grabbed my waist from behind, he began to move at my rhythm, the others celebrated with applause and whistles. I felt how it came back at me from behind, pulling me towards the one held by the waist. Immediately I felt him stop and he gave it to me between my buttocks. I stood up with my ass and moved sexier, rubbing against his cock discreetly of course. However, everyone noticed my movement.

That gave courage to another boy and he joined us in that erotic dance. He stood in front of me and, taking me by the waist, I approached him and he also began to rub my cock from the front. That drove the other kids crazy, who couldn't stop celebrating and applauding.

I was already starting to get horny, with that music, those guys rubbing me with their cocks, I didn't realize or know how , but suddenly I was already touching each of their cocks, one hand in front and the other behind .

They began to grope me more blatantly to the joy of the other boys. One of them lifted my dress, exposing my buttocks, and began to fondle them hornily. The other one who was in front, took my boobies from the bar and started caressing and sucking them. Immediately my nipples stood up and became super hard, like they always do when someone touches me, a sign that I like it and that I'm already horny.

Almost without thinking, I put my hand inside both of their pants, and almost immediately they took off their pants, revealing their cocks, so I proceeded to caress them both very hornily.

Another boy approached and started putting his hand between my legs, touching my sex. He immediately realized that I was already super wet, because of how horny I had gotten. He also quickly took off his pants, lay face up on the carpet and sat me on top of him, inserting his entire cock deep into me, to the joy of the others who couldn't stop celebrating. The other two boys I was with from the beginning began to put his cock in my mouth, taking turns, I grabbed them and sucked them, while the other boy fucked me to his liking.

When I came to tell him, all the boys were already completely naked and were taking turns grabbing their cocks and sucking them, so they all took turns receiving his cock sucked.

Then they took turns making me sit on top of them and put their cock in me, that's how they all went. I never knew for sure if it was 6, 8 or 10 guys who gave me dick that day. The important thing is that I have a wonderful time and of course they do too.

I let myself be fucked by everyone in every position they could think of, taking turns to fuck me. There were incredible moments when they were penetrating me two by two, one from the front and the other from behind and then they took turns so that it was everyone's turn.

We stayed like that for quite a while, take and take, I don't remember how many times I came, but I remember that I enjoyed it like never before.

Finally, they put me on my knees in the center and almost at the same time, they all came in my mouth, on my face, on my tits, in my hair, wherever they touched. It was a wonderful experience, the first time I participated in an orgy, and the truth is...I loved it.

Of course, these meetings were repeated several times, sometimes they brought a girl or another to liven up the meeting more, but usually it was all men.

INFIDELITY WITH MATURE

Since I was young, I always fantasized about the idea that one day, when I was married, I would cheat on my husband with some stranger.

This idea has always been haunting me since I was single.

Now that I'm married, unexpectedly those ideas began to fill my thoughts more and more frequently.

I fantasized imagining myself fucking a stranger and sometimes I even masturbated imagining what that adventure would be like.

I have realized that I have already become a very horny girl, maybe I always was, but now I seem to have it more in mind and the idea of fucking someone other than my husband makes me extremely horny, to the point of I get wet just thinking about those situations.

I always fantasized about it, but now that it was starting to become more real, it kind of made me a little nervous and excited me more than necessary.

So one day, as a joke, I decided to start placing ads on discreet adult pages, the kind where girls offer themselves to men. At the moment all of this seemed fun, horny to me and I masturbated with the idea that one day I would fuck some stranger.

The problem started when someone responded to one of my ads. I didn't expect that, I know that I fantasized about that idea every day, but now, suddenly, there was a stranger writing to me that he wanted to fuck with me, that he had loved my photos and that if I wanted we could meet as soon as possible.

The truth is that it scared me, imagining yourself in bed with another man is not the same as jumping on him in reality, that made me extremely nervous.

So I didn't answer anything. I stayed calm and almost forgot about it, when suddenly I started receiving more response notifications to several of my ads.

That was truly surprising.

Several unknown men wanted to fuck me.

Before they were just my fantasies, but now the opportunity was open to me to make it happen, not with just one, but with whoever I wanted, that made me very restless but also very horny. I had the opportunity to fuck whoever I wanted and all I had to do was accept any of them.

So I started checking the profiles of some of them.

One caught my attention powerfully.

He was an older man, about 65.

You know how mature men are my delirium.

So I read his profile a little more carefully.

If I had any doubts about deciding whether to go out with him, when I read that he weighed 23 cm, well, I no longer hesitated for a moment.

I immediately responded that I was interested.

He seemed surprised because he later confessed that he never imagined I would answer him.

So we met in a neighborhood far from mine, I went in a taxi and arrived at the meeting place.

There he was already, waiting anxiously. So, without further waste of time, I got into his car and we headed to a nearby motel, something very discreet.

Since my story is a bit long, I'll just tell you that the fuck we had exceeded all my expectations.

I had arrived very nervous given the situation, meeting a stranger just so he could put his dick in you, it wasn't anything, of course apart from being nervous, I was super excited and super horny.

Finally, everything went wonderfully, we agreed to meet on other occasions and so we did.

Now, after that incredible experience, I was calmer, I could think better and I definitely decided that I had made an excellent decision, having made my fantasies come true.

With that experience, I kind of allowed myself to plan things better and little by little I began to accept the invitations that came to me from strangers.

With total control, I decided who yes and who no.

So I started accepting invitations from only older men.

The moment came when I thought that I had become not only a real unfaithful and eating whore, but I clearly understood that I was actually a nymphomaniac.

I increasingly needed a stranger's cock. The time came when I was fucking almost daily, that was out of any fantasy I had ever had.

However, I started to get seriously worried when I started to feel the need for not just one cock, but two, or three if possible.

So I started spacing out dates with simple strangers and took on the task of soliciting partners, even if they didn't know each other.

My ad said something like this:

Young dissatisfied married woman available, looking for two mature gentlemen.

For my surprise. The responses came in hundreds almost from the day of the announcement.

So I took on the task of choosing among the applicants.

I was extremely excited by the profiles of two mature men who were already older, they said they were between 70 and 75 but very well endowed ufff.

I immediately responded and we met for our first date.

Needless to say, it was a wonderful experience to fuck with that couple.

They gave me cock for almost 4 hours, I sucked both of them divinely, they fucked me and picked me up to their liking and mine of course, the most incredible and wonderful thing was when they gave me from the front and from behind at the same time.

It was an incredible experience, which, of course, we repeated on several occasions.

This is how my exciting sexual life went on between pairs of cocks, which I enjoyed in an incredible way. I loved the idea of having become an unfaithful nymphomaniac whore.

That single thought excited me tremendously, but I no longer masturbated, I simply just picked up the phone. and ready!!!

END

www.ingramcontent.com/pod-product-compliance
Lightning Source LLC
Chambersburg PA
CBHW022000170726
47994CB00021B/1348